INSECTS FROM OUTER SPACE

Written by
Vladimir Vagin
and
Frank Asch

Illustrated by
Vladimir Vagin

SCHOLASTIC
HARDCOVER

SCHOLASTIC INC.
New York

Library of Congress Cataloging-in-Publication Data
Asch, Frank.
Insects from outer space / written by Frank Asch & Vladimir Vagin;
illustrated by Vladimir Vagin.
p.   cm.
Summary: When bugs from outer space land during the annual Bug Ball,
the earth bugs are initially frightened but eventually invite them to stay for the dancing
and the crowning of the King and Queen Bug.
ISBN 0-590-45489-7
[1. Insects — Fiction. 2. Extraterrestrial beings — Fiction.
3. Balls (Parties) — Fiction.] I. Vagin, Vladimir Vasil'evich,
1937—   . II. Title. PZ7.A778In 1995 [E]—dc20   93-26876
CIP
AC
12 11 10 9 8 7 6 5 4 3 2 1   5 6 7 8 9/9 0/0
Printed in the U.S.A.   37
First printing, April 1995
Mr. Vagin's pictures were drawn first in pencil
and then painted in watercolor.

To Claire,
of course.
F.A.

Several times in my life,
I have seen unusual phenomena
in the sky. This book is for all
who believe in miracles.
And to the little boy,
Samuel.
V.V.

"**D**ANCING is for sissy bugs," said my best friend Hercules when I told him I was going to the annual Bug Ball.

"You're just saying that because you dance like a dead leaf blowing in the wind!" I said.

"Maybe so, but you can't take two steps without tripping on your antennae," replied Hercules.

Hercules was right. But I knew a certain yellow butterfly was going to be at the Bug Ball. I wasn't planning on asking her to dance. That would be too bold. I just wanted to watch her glide across the ballroom floor.

I said goodbye to Hercules and flew from our tiny island to the beach where the ball was to be held. Insects from miles around were gathered there.

While they ate and drank and visited with one another,
the musicians tuned up for the big event: the dance contest
to decide who would be King and Queen Bug of the Ball.

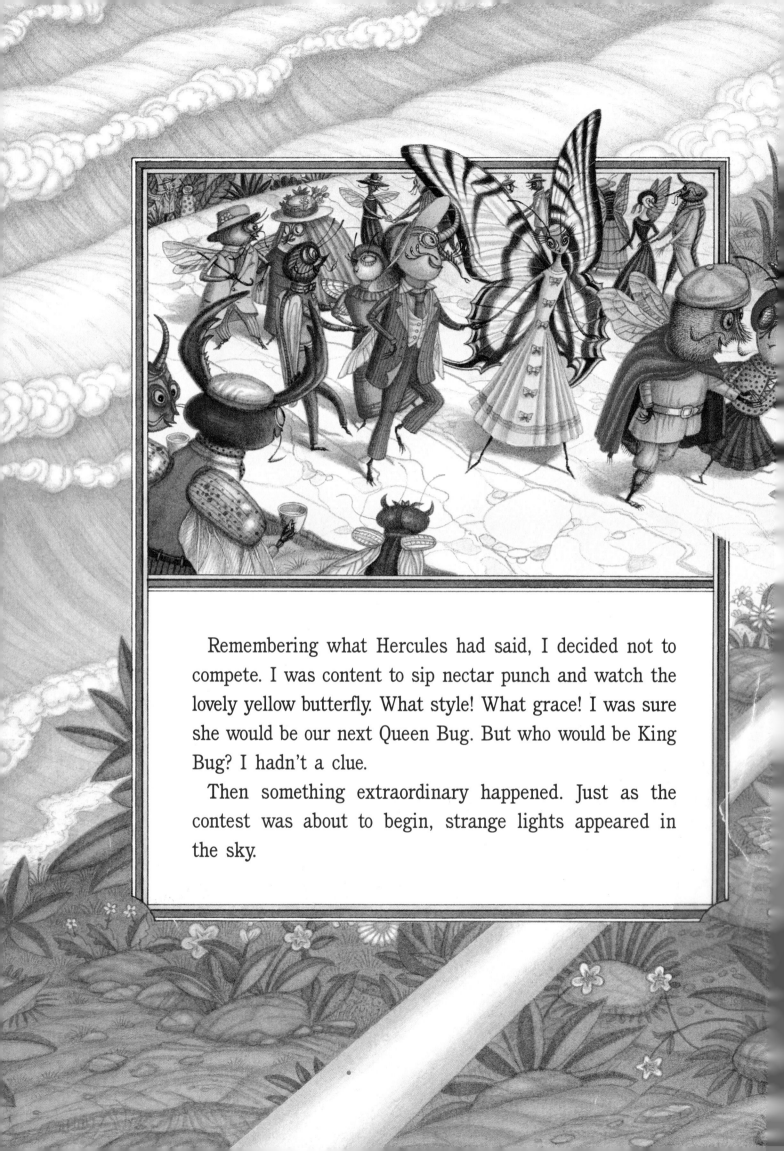

Remembering what Hercules had said, I decided not to compete. I was content to sip nectar punch and watch the lovely yellow butterfly. What style! What grace! I was sure she would be our next Queen Bug. But who would be King Bug? I hadn't a clue.

Then something extraordinary happened. Just as the contest was about to begin, strange lights appeared in the sky.

The lights grew brighter and brighter. Spellbound, we watched them change into a gigantic flower and land on the island where Hercules and I live.

"Run for your lives!" someone cried. "We're being invaded by insects from outer space!"

Like everyone else, I fled. But while they flew away from the strange spaceship, I rushed toward it. Hercules was all by himself on our island. I had to save him from those weird invaders.

I flew as fast as my wings would carry me. But when I arrived, Hercules had already made friends with the insects from outer space.

"These are really smart bugs," said Hercules. "I've only just met them and already they know our language!"

"We're stopping on your planet for a rest," said the three-headed captain of the alien spaceship. "We are very interested in native customs. Though our visit will be brief, we would like to learn as much as possible about your planet."

"Too bad everyone got frightened and ran away. We could have taken you to the Bug Ball," I said.

"Maybe with your help we can invite them back," replied the Spacebug Captain.

The insects from another planet took us inside their spaceship.

"BLAST OFF!" commanded the Spacebug Captain, and we wove a giant spider's web in the sky.

"Now. Tell us what to write in the web," said the Spacebug Captain.

"Okay," replied Hercules. "Write: *Don't be afraid. We want to be friends.*"

And I added, *"Let's dance!"*

The aliens gave us a ride back to the ball.

One by one, our bugs came out of hiding. It was a tense moment but soon everyone was rubbing antennae and shaking feelers.

The spacebugs ate some of our food and we ate some of theirs. After a while their musicians and our musicians started making music together.

When the sun set, the Spacebug Captain said, "Time for us to go now."

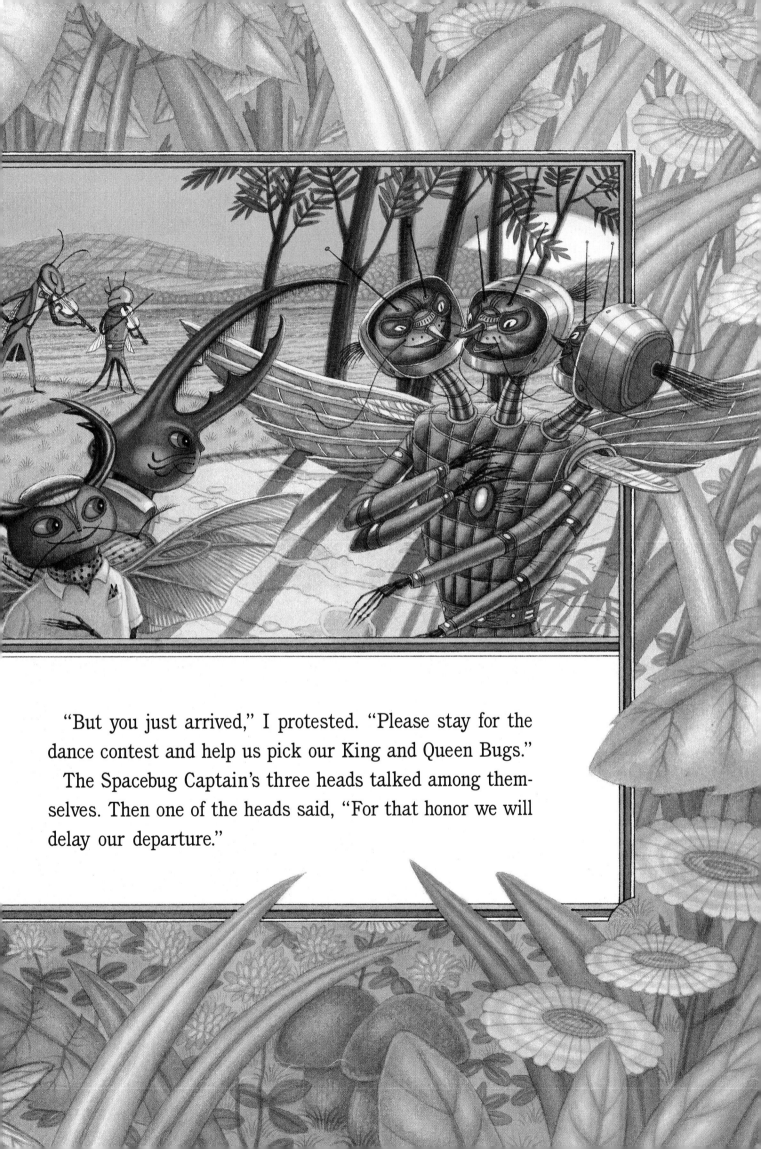

"But you just arrived," I protested. "Please stay for the dance contest and help us pick our King and Queen Bugs."

The Spacebug Captain's three heads talked among themselves. Then one of the heads said, "For that honor we will delay our departure."

When the contest finally began, Hercules turned to leave.
"Dancing. Pooh!" he said. "This is where I go home!"
"But look how the aliens dance," I whispered in
Hercules's ear hole.

Hercules watched the aliens jitterbugging on the dance floor. His eyes bugged out.

"Why, they dance just like you and me!" he cried.

"Only worse!" I said. We both jumped onto the dance floor and kicked up our appendages.

When the contest was over, the lovely yellow butterfly was chosen to be our Queen. No surprise there, but guess what? I was crowned King Bug!

It was the happiest moment of my life.

But now the time had come for the insects from outer space to go home.

"It was a great pleasure to meet earth bugs," said the Spacebug Captain. "Wherever we go in the universe, we will always praise your planet."

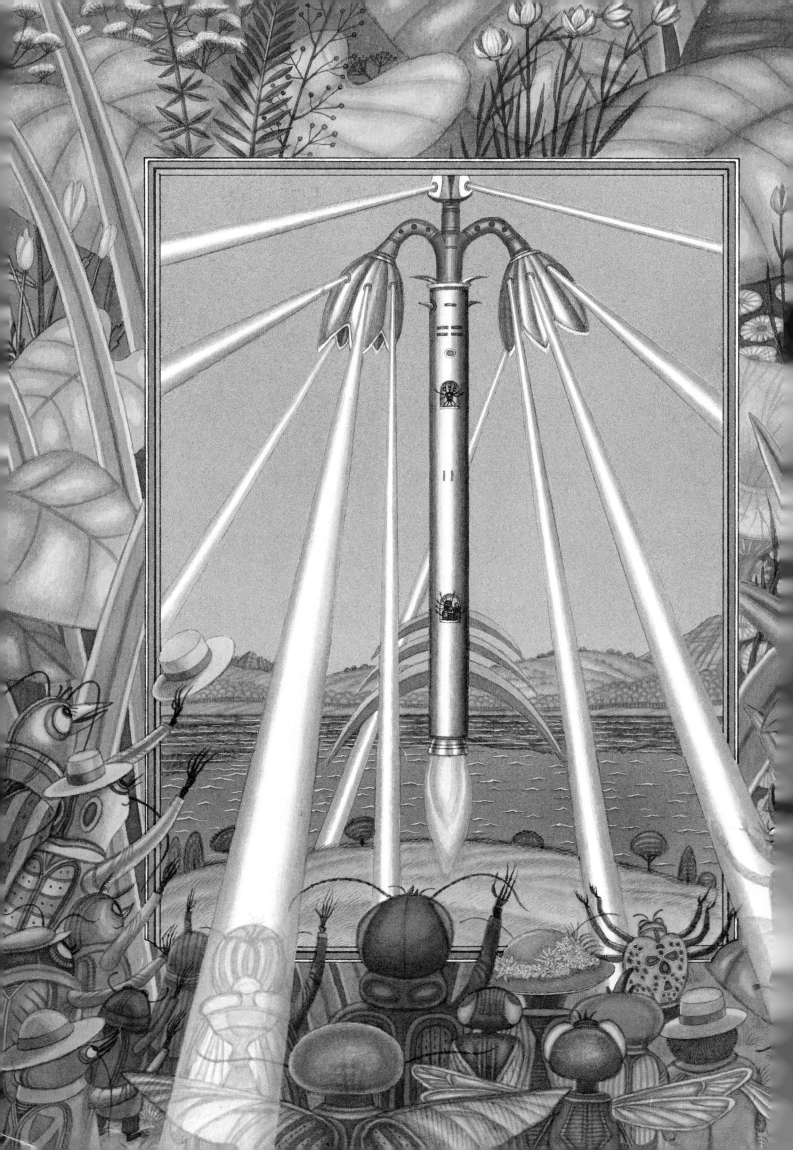

We said goodbye to our new friends and watched their spaceship slowly lift off into the night sky.

Then, as King and Queen Bug, the lovely yellow butterfly and I led the last dance, to officially end the annual Bug Ball.

What a thrill it was to hold the lovely yellow butterfly.

"I love the way you dance," I told her.

"And your dancing is out of this world!" she replied.